CONTENTS

think POSITIVE

Published 2020.

Little Brother Books, Ground Floor,
23 Southernhay East, Exeter, Devon, EX1 1QL

Printed in Poland.

books@littlebrotherbooks.co.uk |
www.littlebrotherbooks.co.uk

The Little Brother Books trademark, email
and website addresses and the Pop Winners
logo and imprint are sole and exclusive
properties of Little Brother Books Limited.

Images used under license from Shutterstock.com

NO BAD VIBES

All about JESY

FULL NAME: Jessica Louise Nelson
DATE OF BIRTH: 14th June, 1991
STAR SIGN: Gemini
HOME TOWN: Romford
FAVE COLOURS: Red and black

TOP MEAL

She's the takeaway queen and a spicy curry is always top of Jesy's menu. Who doesn't love a good ruby?

Most listened to album or song

- ♥ Respect ⇨ Missy Elliot,
- ♥ 4 ⇨ Beyoncé
- ♥ F.A.M.E. ⇨ Chris Brown

STYLE ICON

Jesy thinks Gwen Stefani's nailed the aesthetic with her original outfits and unique style. Gwen isn't afraid to go bold which is a lewk Jesy wears well too.

Rock

MUSICAL INSPO
Jesy totes adores hip hop superstar Missy Elliot. The multi-talented singer/rapper/dancer/song-writer is one of her idols.

If Jesy was an emoji she would be:

LOVES TATTOOS

HATES GREASY FOOD

All about LEIGH-ANNE

FULL NAME: Leigh-Anne Pinnock
DATE OF BIRTH: 4th October, 1991
STAR SIGN: Libra
HOME TOWN: High Wycombe
FAVE COLOUR: Green

TOP MEAL

Tex Mex inspired nachos is Leigh-Anne's meal of choice. With all the trimmings obvs.

Most listened to album or song

- Who You Are ➡ Jessie J
- Music Box ➡ Mariah Carey
- U Got It Bad ➡ Usher

STYLE ICON

Stylish Rihanna is Leigh-Anne's fashion kweeeen. Rih-Rih wears her clothes with confidence, just like our Leigh-Anne.

Did You Know?

Leigh-Anne was a pom pom waving cheerleader in primary school. All together now, 'Gimme an L...'

MUSICAL INSPO

When she was little it was American diva Mariah Carey who first made Leigh-Anne want to sing. And thank goodness she did!

ROCK

If Leigh-Anne was an emoji she would be:

LOVES
JUSTIN BIEBER

HATES
LONDON DRIVERS

All about PERRIE

FULL NAME: Perrie Edwards
DATE OF BIRTH: 10th July, 1993
STAR SIGN: Cancer
HOME TOWN: South Shields
FAVE COLOUR: Blue

TOP MEAL

Perrie loves the Northern classic mince with dumplings and is rather partial to spaghetti and meatballs. Mmmm, we're getting hungry just thinking about it...

Most listened to album or song

♥ Britney Spears ⇨ Greatest Hits
♥ Journey ⇨ Greatest Hits

STYLE ICON

Perrie looks to Mary Kate and Ashley for style inspo. She thinks the Olsen sisters would slay in anything they wore.

Did You Know?
Perrie's fave item of clothing is the versatile headband.
She's lost count of how many she owns.

LETHING

MIX

ROCK

MUSICAL INSPO

Home girl Pez like to keep it in the family when it comes to musical inspiration. She thinks her singing parents are the most talented people she knows. How adorbs is that?

If Perrie was an emoji she would be:

LOVES
JAPAN

HATES
PUTTING RUBBISH OUT

All about JADE

FULL NAME: Jade Thirlwall
DATE OF BIRTH: 26th December, 1992
STAR SIGN: Capricorn
HOME TOWN: South Shields
FAVE COLOURS: Teal, purple and gold

TOP MEAL

Jade loves a cracking Sunday roast as it reminds her of being at home with her fam - awww! She's also rather keen on that Italian classic, lasagne - homemade by her Mam, of course!

Most listened to album or song

- *Back to Black* ⇒ Amy Winehouse
- *Sigh No More* ⇒ Mumford & Sons
- *Redemption Song* ⇒ Beyoncé and Eddie Vedder.

STYLE ICON

Jade thinks Alexa Chung's effortlessly cool look is totally trending. She'd love to steal her style.

MUSICAL INSPO

As a young girl, wannabe singer Jade adored Diana Ross. She used to love watching her videos and copying all her dance moves.

If Jade was an emoji she would be:

LOVES
LIQUID EYELINER

HATES
CLOWNS

STATUS:

Celeb

OMG! Little Mix have chosen YOU as their new fifth member! Once you've picked yourself up off the floor, create your own popstar profile below.

Your **LEWK IS...**

Stick a selfie here or doodle a self-portrait.

THE GIRLS' NICKNAME FOR YOU IS...

Design yo'self some fierce threads!

Your awards ceremony dress is...

☐   ☐   ☐   ☐

Your popstar pad is

A HOLLYWOOD MANSION ☐
A COUNTRY RETREAT ☐
A LONDON LOFT APARTMENT ☐

IN THE GROUP YOU'RE THE...

CHATTERBOX ☐
CONFIDENT ONE ☐
JOKER ☐
THOUGHTFUL ONE ☐
BUBBLY ONE ☐

YOUR BAND BFF IS...

JESY ☐   LEIGH-ANNE ☐   JADE ☐   PERRIE ☐   ALL OF THEM, OF COURSE! ☐

Changes CHALLENGE

Little Mix are posing for the paps. How quickly can you spot the 10 differences between these two pics? Time yourself then rate your skills. #ChallengeAccepted

How'd Ya Do?

 **LESS THAN 2 MINUTES** Smashed it!

 2 TO 4 MINUTES Meh!

 **MORE THAN 4 MINUTES** Epic fail!

Answers on pages 76-77.

Little Mix
LOOK BACK

With awards to be won, songs to release and festivals to perform at, the girls are always on the go. Let's take a look at some of the recent highlights from Planet Little Mix.

PERF PERFORMANCE

Little Mix fans were super excited to see the fab four pop up on the final of *The Voice Kids UK*. The girls looked like they were feeling all sorts of happy as they performed *Bounce Back* to the screaming crowd.

GO JESY!

Jesy was delighted to nab the award for best factual programme at the 2020 National Television Awards for her documentary *Odd One Out*. In the heartbreakingly honest doc, Jesy explored the effects that cyberbullying has on mental health and opened up about the online bullying she received during her first few years in Little Mix. What an inspo for fans everywhere.

WHAT WOULD YOU GIVE JESY'S AWARD-WINNING DOC OUT OF 10?

AMAZING MENTOR

Jesy got to relive her *X Factor* days when she was invited to be a guest mentor on *The Voice UK*. Joining Will.i.am to help choose his semi-finalists, Jesy found out what things were like on the other side of the mic.

WIN AND REPEAT

Little Mix added another award to their trophy cabinet when they bagged Best UK and Ireland Act in the 2019 MTV European Music Awards. And it isn't the first time the girls have received this honour – they also won the title in 2018, 2016 and 2015. Should they let someone else have a turn next year? Err, no!

WHO WOULD YOU CHOOSE AS YOUR LITTLE MIX MENTOR?

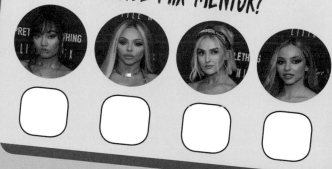

BRAZIL DEBUT

The girls headed to South America to headline at Festival GRLS 2020 in Brazil. They smashed it with an epic 14-song set list, despite being a member down as poor Perrie was ill. Bad timing, Pez!

WHAT SONG WOULD YOU MOST LIKE TO SEE LITTLE MIX PERFORM?

Sweet Melody

BEACH LIFE

Leigh-Anne's swimwear range In 'A' Seashell continues to boss beach fashion. Designed with real people in mind, lovely Leigh hopes anyone can wear and feel good in her bold bikinis, whatever their body shape. Here she is chatting on TV show *Lorraine*, while modelling one of her creations in the background.

LOCKDOWN SHOW

In the midst of the global Coronavirus pandemic, Little Mix performed during lockdown from their separate homes for *One World: Together at Home*. The tribute show to celebrate key workers was watched by six million people in the UK. As well as giving a heartfelt rendition of *Touch*, fans got a rare sneaky peek inside the girls' houses. Ooooh!

ONE WORLD **TOGETHER AT HOME**

GLOBAL CITIZEN — World Health Organization

TELLY TIME

Gogglebox fans were happy to see Little Mix throw on their comfy clothes and put their feet up in front of the telly in *Celebrity Gogglebox 2019*. The girls added their own hilare commentary to popular TV shows and Perrie's pet pooch even made an appearance.

FESTIVAL FEVER

Little Mix rocked the main stage at Fusion Festival 2019 in Liverpool's Sefton Park. The two-day event lived up to its promise to be bigger and better than ever before, with the likes of Rudimental, Dizzee Rascal and Jonas Blue joining the girls at the star-studded extravaganza.

LM MERCH

Little Mix love their merch and were proud to team up with LGBT charity Stonewall to create a range of Pride products. Poppin' with the statement 'Love who you wanna', the rainbow themed tees and sweatshirts were totally on point.

PLAN B

The Little Mixers claimed their 15th top 10 hit when single *Break Up Song* was released. And after the girls were forced to cancel their shoot for the official video due to the Coronavirus lockdown, they quickly came up with a plan b and produced a video in felt form! The quirky production saw animated versions of the girls hosting their own breakfast TV show, *LMTV*, complete with weather forecasts, aerobic workouts and awesome 80s outfits. Full marks for making the best of a bad situation, girls.

WHICH EMOJI WOULD YOU AWARD THE BREAK UP SONG VIDEO?

☐ ☐ ☐

HOT LIKE WASABI

Two years after releasing the song *Wasabi* on the *LM5* album, Little Mix finally got around to making a video for this fan fave. Made up of a montage of behind-the-scenes clips from their LM5 tour, the fast-paced vid was totally worth the wait.

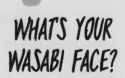

WHAT'S YOUR WASABI FACE?

 ♡ ☐

FAN POWER

Everyone knows that Little Mix are the best group on the entire planet and now they have the award to prove it! The singing sensations scooped the Best Group gong at the Radio 1 Teen Awards 2019. And this award is extra spesh as it's voted for by the public. Another victory for Little Mix's army of fans!

DID YOU VOTE FOR LITTLE MIX?

YES ☑   NO ☐

PARTY TIME!

The girls got their fash on when they launched a partywear collection with PrettyLittleThing. The bold range, featuring snake print, denim, sequins and faux fur, is guaranteed to slay!

WHAT'S YOUR PARTYWEAR STYLE?

BRIGHT AND BOLD ☐

SPARKLY AND SHINY ☒

COMFY AND CASUAL ☒

WHO ARE YOU?

Which Little Mix member are you most like?
Pick your fave thing in each category to find out!

FOOD

CURRY A	ROAST DINNER B	NACHOS C	MEATBALLS D

FOOTWEAR

HIGH-TOPS A	HEELS B	BOOTS C	SNEAKERS D

COLOUR

RED A	PURPLE B	GREEN C	BLUE D

HOBBY

WATCHING TV A	PAINTING B	WRITING SONGS C	KNITTING D

DRINK

COLA A	TEA B	HOT CHOCOLATE C	SMOOTHIE D

RESULTS

MOSTLY BLUE
JESY
You're bold and brave and aren't afraid to speak your mind - you and Jesy could be twins!

MOSTLY ORANGE
JADE
You're totally Jade - kind, thoughtful and sweet. You two would make great mates.

MOSTLY RED
LEIGH-ANNE
You're cool and confident on the outside and warm and caring on the inside - just like Leigh-Anne!

MOSTLY GREEN
PERRIE
You're so Perrie - bubbly, funny and always up for a laff. You and Pez should hang out sometime!

24

What do you MEME?

Here's one to get you going...

Turn up the silly and add your own hilare captions to these Little Mix pix. It's all about the LOLs!

WHEN YOU REALISE THAT YOU'VE STOLEN YOUR DANCE MOVES FROM 'I'M A LITTLE TEAPOT'.

#TOTALLY TRENDING

The Little Mix girls are kweens of the socials. Scroll down to read some of their top tweets.

10

Jesy, Perrie and Jade were feeling all sorts of happy when they announced Leigh-Anne's engagement to footballer Andre Gray. Awww!

Little Mix ✔
@LittleMix

Our beautiful girl is ENGAGED 🖤 Our hearts are full for you and Andre. Wishing you a life time of happiness together 🥰🥰 Love you, the girls xx

9

The girls got nostalgic with this tweet to celebrate five years of Black Magic.

Little Mix ✔
@LittleMix

Black Magic, five years old today 🔮🖤 Time has flownnnn by!! Thank you to every one of you for all the love you've shown this song. Can't wait to sing it with you again someday soon

8

Little Mix were missing each other during the coronavirus lockdown as this heartfelt message shows.

Little Mix ✔
@LittleMix

We've been getting all kindsa soppy in our group chat reminiscing and saying how much we miss each other! Can't wait to be in the same room vibing, singing and laughing together again 💕 the girls xx

 95 🖤

7

Leigh-Anne gave a shout out to women everywhere on the day of the BRIT Awards. #GirlsAreAwesome

Little Mix ✔
@LittleMix

Whose excited for the @BRITs tonight? So good to see the genre diversity with some influential grime artists nominated. But there are so many female bosses who aren't up, come on @brits where's the ladies at? So many are smashing it right now! Ladies we see u! 🖤 Leigh x

28

6

An emotional Jesy thanked fans after winning a National Television Award for her awesome documentary *Odd One Out*.

Little Mix ✔
@LittleMix

I woke up this morning and my heart is bursting with happiness! I can't thank you enough for making this moment happen, there are no words to describe how this moment felt - you guys made this one of the most magical nights of my life! I love you all so much thank you 🖤

 60 ♥

5

On NYE, Little Mix said goodbye to 2019 with a special thank you to their fans.

Little Mix ✔
@LittleMix

We love you guys so much, we say it all the time but for real... WE REALLY DO! Thank you for an amazing 2019, you guys are such a dream! Here's to 2020 ⭐ 🖤

4

After winning a Radio One Teen Award, the girls gave a shout out to all the Mixers who voted for them. #SmashedIt

Little Mix ✔
@LittleMix

We did it!!! YOU DID IT! Thank you so much, we love you more than words can say (literally) thank you @BBCR1 💕 #R1TeenAwards

3

Feeling totes emotional at the end of the LM5 tour, Little Mix had this to say.

Little Mix ✔
@LittleMix

You guys have been absolutely incredible on #LM5TheTour. Performing each night has been A DREAM! thank you to every single person involved and every single person who came to the shows. We can't thank you enough 🙏

82 ♥

2

A proud Leigh-Anne bigged up the inspirational women who featured in her new swimwear campaign.

Little Mix ✔
@LittleMix

Super excited for my new campaign for @inaseashell #LIKESEASHELLS I am so in awe of these incredible women who have been brave enough to speak about their journeys to self love! Full campaign drops 4th November! ☀️🌴🖤

1

A red-faced Jade commented on this hilare tweet from a LM fan.

Little Mix ✔
@LittleMix

Absolutely mortified 😂 jade x

David Dodd @dpdy2k · Nov 19, 2019
Favourite moment in @LittleMix #LM5TheTourLeeds #LM5TheTour tonight....Jade dropping her microphone on the floor, picking it up and then singing into the wrong end! 😂 Wish id got it on video!

Whose WARDROBE?

Can you identify Little Mix by their outfits alone? Get your fash on and work out which clothes collection belongs to which Mixer.

Wardrobe:

Wardrobe:

Wardrobe:

Wardrobe:

Wardrobe A

HUN

Wardrobe B   Wardrobe C   Wardrobe D

BALENCIAGA

MOSCHINO

SO INSPO

Let's take a closer look at some of the amazing women who've inspired Jesy, Leigh-Anne, Perrie and Jade to be their best selves!

MARVELLOUS MUNROE

Model and activist Munroe Bergdorf is a huge inspo for Jade. On International Women's Day (IWD) 2020, Jade tweeted, "I feel like Munroe really isn't afraid to fight the good fight, which is so inspiring for somebody like me". We can feel the love from here!

love you

INSPIRING RENI

It's journalist, author and podcaster Reni Eddo-Lodge who Leigh-Anne looks to for inspiration. In a tweet on IWD 2020, Leigh-Anne said, "Reni Eddo-Lodge's courage and power to speak up and effortlessly put into words what racial discrimination feels and looks like has changed my life". Enough said, we think.

FEARLESS FELICITY

On IWD 2020, Jesy chose model and body positive activist Felicity Hayward as her inspo. "I love that she reps it for the curvy women", Jesy tweeted. Well said, Jes! Everyone should feel that they can wear what they want, regardless of body shape or size.

SUPERSTAR RIHANNA

Leigh-Anne looks to R&B singing sensation Rihanna as her musical icon and we can see why. With an amazing voice that's totally versatile, you never know what Rihanna is gonna offer up next. Oh, and her wardrobe is pretty fierce too!

I LOVE YOU

AMAZING MISSY

When it comes to musical influences, Jesy thinks Missy Elliott bosses it. The R&B superstar teamed up with the girls in their first collaboration *How Ya Doin'?* way back in 2013 and has continued to inspire Jesy ever since.

BRILLIANT BEYONCE

Perrie can't get enough of ballad blasting Beyoncé and names the songstress as a HUGE inspo. Bey first found fame with girl group *Destiny's Child* before becoming a solo star. Please don't get any ideas about following in her footsteps and abandoning Little Mix, Pez!

ICONIC DIANA

Since she was a little girl, Jade has been inspired by musical legend Diana Ross. She may be well into her 70s but the world famous diva still knows how to work a crowd! Will Little Mix still be performing at her age? We really, really hope so!

Answers on pages 76-77.

X WORD FUN!

Test your Little Mix knowledge with this crossword all about your faves.

Answers on pages 76-77.

DOWN

1. Jade's hometown (5, 7).

2. Perrie's fave colour (4).

3. _ _ _ _ / _ _ _ _ _ _ UK, the music talent show Jesy was a guest mentor on (3, 5).

4. _ _ _ _ _ _ Ross, the legendary American diva Jade grew up listening to (5).

5. Body positive activist and Jesy's inspo, _ _ _ _ _ _ _ _ Hayward (8).

ACROSS

1. The name of Jesy's award-winning documentary (3, 3, 3).

2. The girls' first animated video made during lockdown (5, 2, 4).

3. This video was filmed backstage on the LM5 tour (6).

4. The name of Leigh-Anne's swimwear range (2, 1, 8).

5. _ _ _ _ _ _ Elliott, who the girls collaborated with on *How Ya Doin'*? (5).

PSSSSST!

If you need a bit of help, all of the answers can be found somewhere in this book.

THE LM5 TOUR

Flash your Access All Areas pass to take a peek behind the scenes of Little Mix's sell-out tour!

INTRODUCING LM5

Back in 2019, the girls packed their bags and hopped on their tour bus for Little Mix's sixth tour, LM5. The 40-show musical extravaganza was a hit-blasting, costume-changing, dance-crazy celebration of their fifth album of the same name.

SUPER SET LIST

Barely pausing for breath, the Mixers belted out hit after hit. The 20-song set list included powerful anthems like *Salute*, *Woman Like Me* and *The National Manthem*, as well as more recent hits like *Bounce Back*, classics like *Shout Out to My Ex* and blasts from the past such as *Wings*. The girls were even joined on stage by Stormzy to perform *Power* at two of the London dates.

FILMING FUN

Somehow in the midst of this cray tour, the girls even managed to find time to film a music video for their much-loved song *Wasabi*. The tongue-in-cheek vid features behind-the-scenes footage of the girls on their tour bus, in their dressing room and strutting their stuff down various corridors. There are also pillow fights, cute kids, the Eiffel Tower and an appearance from Jesy's boyf at the time, Chris Hughes. What more could you want from a music video?

BUSY SCHEDULE

The tour kicked off in Madrid, Spain, in September and finished in London's O2 in November. In between the girls played to packed-out arenas in Italy, Germany, Netherlands, Belgium and France on the Europe leg, before heading home for the UK leg, which also took in Dublin, Belfast, Glasgow, Liverpool, Newcastle, Sheffield, Birmingham, Nottingham, Manchester and Leeds. Phew, we're exhausted just thinking about it!

SLAYING THE SHOW

True to form, the girls put on a powerful, entertaining show with amazing choreography and extraordinary vocals. To add a bit of extra awesomeness (as if they needed it!) there was even a rain machine, pyrotechnics and a moving platform that flew above the audience. Oh, and we mustn't forget the slogans of female empowerment that appeared throughout the show – so inspo.

RECORD BREAKERS

The tour was completely sold out and the girls managed to break a record in Glasgow for selling more tickets than any other artist at The SSE Hydro. Fans screamed with delight as Jade thanked them from the stage for helping them smash sales for three nights in a row. How. Awesome. Is. That.

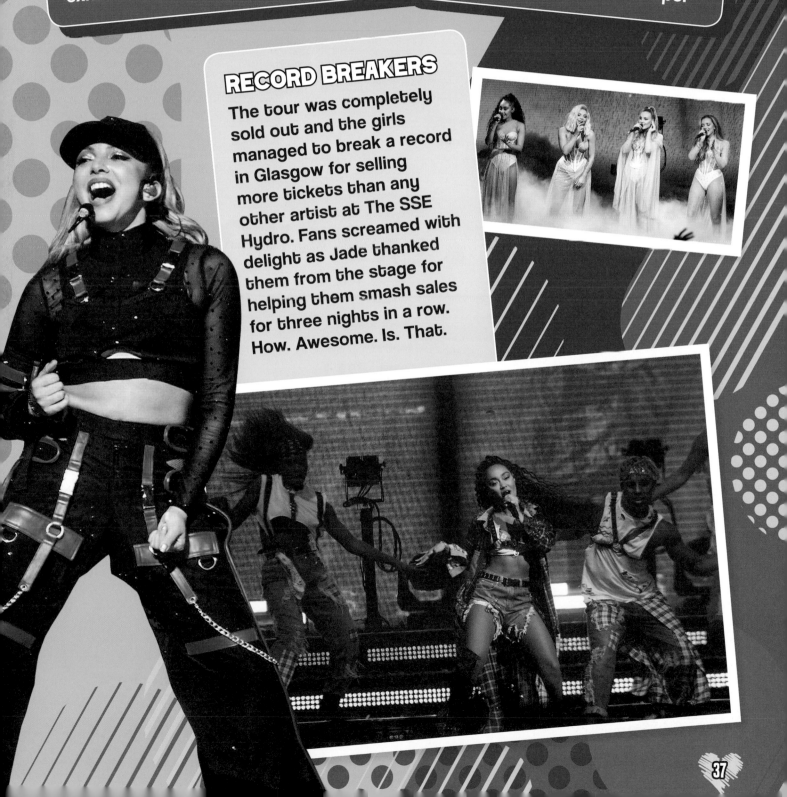

Song SCRAMBLE

How quickly can you unscramble these Little Mix song titles? #TheClockIsTicking

1. SBAIWA

_ _ _ _ _ _

2. OMWNA KEIL EM

_ _ _ _ _ / _ _ _ _ / _ _

3. REWPO

_ _ _ _ _

4. LABKC ICGAM

_ _ _ _ _ / _ _ _ _ _

5. TKINH BOAUT SU

_ _ _ _ _ / _ _ _ _ _ / _ _

6. ONCBUE CKAB

_ _ _ _ _ _ / _ _ _ _

7. LYNO OUY

_ _ _ _ / _ _ _

8. ON REOM DAS GSSON

_ _ / _ _ _ _ / _ _ _ / _ _ _ _ _

Answers on pages 76-77.

Video BINGO!

Grab a friend to play this fun game. It's the perfect excuse to watch back-to-back Little Mix videos (as if you needed one).

HOW TO PLAY

1. Cut out your bingo cards - if you don't want to cut up your book, photocopy the cards or scan and print.

2. Choose a bingo card each then watch a Little Mix video. If something written on your bingo card happens in the video, cross out that box.

3. Keep watching videos until someone gets a line (three boxes in a row, either down, across or diagonally).

4. If you want to carry on, keep watching videos until someone gets a full house - that's bingo lingo for crossing off every box on your card!

PLAYER 1

SOMEONE **POINTS** DIRECTLY AT THE **CAMERA**.	YOU **HEAR** THE WORD **LOVE**.	SOMEONE **BLOWS** A **KISS**.
PERRIE STICKS HER **TONGUE** OUT.	SOMEONE **FLUTTERS** THEIR **EYELASHES**.	THE **GIRLS** HAVE AN **OUTFIT** CHANGE.
SOMETHING GETS **THROWN** IN THE **AIR**.	YOU **SPOT** A **HOTTIE**!	SOMEONE **NODS** IN TIME **TO** THE **MUSIC**.

PLAYER 2

JESY FLICKS **HER** HAIR.	SOMEONE **WAGGLES** THEIR **FINGER**.	YOU SEE AN **OUTFIT** YOU **WANT**.
SOMEONE **WALKS** WITH A **WIGGLE**.	**JESY** RAISES HER **EYEBROWS**.	SOMEONE **WINKS**.
LEIGH-ANNE **TWIRLS** HER **CURLS**.	YOU **HEAR** THE WORD **GIRL**.	SOMEONE **RAISES** AN **ARM** IN THE **AIR**.

Before they WERE FAMOUS

It's hard to think of Little Mix as anything other than world famous popstars, but once Leigh-Anne, Perrie, Jesy and Jade were just normal girls with big dreams.

HOME LIFE

They might be A-listers now, but all four girls came from more humble roots. Jade describes her fam as, "a typical normal family, living in a terraced house". Leigh-Anne shared a room with one of her two sisters and Jesy's home was "a bit of a madhouse" as she has two brothers and a sister all quite close in age. Perrie grew up with her mam and big brother, or 'The Three Amigos' as she calls them.

Before they were famous famous!

The Three Amigos

FRIENDS

Cut back to the early noughties and like most teenage girls, the Mixers each had their own group of core school friends. And they did all the stuff that you probably do with your BFFs! Amazingly they're still besties with their childhood friends today. Leigh-Anne says of her home buddies, "I adore them; they'd do anything for me."

A bit of a swot!

Super fast sprinter Jesy!

HOBBIES

Like lots of teens, the girls had after-school and weekend hobbies. Leigh-Anne had singing lessons, played piano for a year and had a drum kit for a while. And Jesy used to go to theatre school on a Saturday to do drama, dancing and singing. But it wasn't all about being on stage, another of Jesy's hobbies was sprinting. She used to be a bit of a champion but had to give it up because the sound of the starting gun scared her! Bless.

SCHOOL

You may well imagine the teenage Little Mixers singing their hearts out at stage school but in fact, apart from Jesy, the girls all went to normal secondary schools. Jade was "a bit of a swot", Leigh-Anne was "never part of the cool crowd" and Perrie was "never very academic". Bet they all enjoyed their music lessons though!

JOBS

Before getting THE BEST JOB IN THE WORLD the Little Mixers tried their hands at other professions. Jesy had a job behind a bar and Leigh-Anne worked as a waitress in Pizza Hut during her gap year. But the girls were always hoping for bigger things. "All this time I was writing music and dreaming of being a singer," says Leigh-Anne.

Pizza anyone?

All quotes are taken from the official biography _Little Mix Our World_.

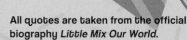

MIX Makeover

This is not a drill – Little Mix want you to be their new celeb stylist! Can you design a fierce new look for each of the girls?

Why not add an embellishment?

INSPO **alert**

Use the fab fabrics on these pages to inspire your design.

Body CONFIDENCE

You're Great

Learn to celebrate your uh-mazing body, just like Jesy, Jade, Leigh-Anne and Perrie have done!

your self

BE YOU TIFUL

Learning Journey

When you see Little Mix in their fierce clothes, dancing their hearts out on stage and loving every minute of it, it's hard to imagine them as anything other than 100% happy with their bodies. But there have been times when the girls haven't been totally body confident.

Jade has suffered from anorexia, Jesy was bullied at school for how she looked, Leigh-Anne has dealt with racism because of the colour of her skin and Perrie has felt self-conscious about her freckles and the scar on her stomach from surgery as a child.

However you feel about your body, there are things you can do to build confidence in how you look, celebrate your fabulous self and learn to love your bod – just like the Leigh-Anne, Jesy, Perrie and Jade have.

5 ways to BUILD BODY CONFIDENCE

1 Remember that every body is different. There isn't a right size, shape or colour.

2 Take exercise to get to know your body and what it can do. Start with something gentle like stretching or yoga and work up from there.

3 When it comes to clothes, create your own style that you feel comfortable with. Be the real you.

4 Try to focus on the parts of your body you like rather than the bits you're not so keen on.

5 Look in the mirror and say:

MY BODY IS GOOD.

MY BODY IS STRONG.

MY BODY CAN DO INCREDIBLE THINGS.

BEE KIND

UH-MAZING ME!

Write a list of some of the things that make you great – both inside and out.

Rate It or SLATE IT?

You can't have a hit song without a killer music video! Over to you to rate some of Little Mix's best known vids.

OVER TO YOU!
Give each LM video a rating.

Love, love, love it!   Hmmm, it's OK.   Soz, it's a no from me.

BREAK UP SONG

Little Mix's first animated video shows the girls hosting their own breakfast TV show, *LMTV*. A felt version of Leigh-Anne is checking out the headlines, Jesy's giving the weather forecast, Perrie's leading an aerobic workout and Jade's gazing into a crystal ball. And just when you think things can't get any better, the girls appear IRL, dressed in supercool 80s outfits for *LMTV*'s 'live performance'!

BLACK MAGIC

One of the best things about Little Mix is they don't take themselves too seriously and the *Black Magic* video totally proves that. Set in a cliquey high school, the girls transform themselves from geeks to goddesses with the help of a magic book and a secret potion. There's even a cringe moment when they use their powers to make one of the school's mean girls parp in front of the hot boys!

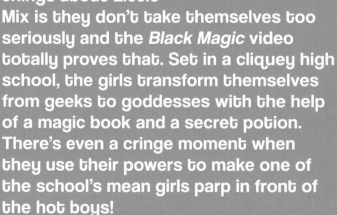

BOUNCE BACK

Bounce Back begins with a little girl opening up her dolls house to play, and guess who's inside? Leigh-Anne, Jade, Perrie and Jesy as dolls obvs! There's also a unicorn, fierce leopard print outfits and a whole load of dancing (Leigh-Anne bosses at twerking btw!). And the ending is adorbs. The look on the girl's face when she notices her dolls are actually alive...

WOMAN LIKE ME

We love this hilare video that sees the girls taking it out of traditionally female roles. At the beginning they're trying to be elegant ladies (walking with books balanced on their heads, practising eating daintily, arranging flowers) but by the end they're stuffing their faces and smashing stuff! And Nicki Minaj appearing as a rapping portrait takes it to a whole other level!

NO MORE SAD SONGS

Little Mix went all cowgirl on us in the video for *No More Sad Songs*! Set in a country and western saloon, the fun vid shows the girls slaying cowboy hats, line dancing and riding bucking broncos. Yee-ha! And it all goes a little cray cray at the end with Leigh-Anne, Perrie, Jade and Jesy spraying everyone with soda water! How do they pack so much awesomeness into four minutes?

10 Reasons why LM ARE TOTALLY relatable

Don't let the sell-out concerts, chart-topping choons and red carpet appearances fool you - Little Mix are really just like you!

1 THEY EAT AT CHAIN RESTAURANTS

It's no secret that Jesy loves Nandos (she always has a quarter chicken with lemon and herbs, chips and rice in case you're wondering) and she's rather partial to a Domino's pepperoni pizza too.

2 THEY WATCH TRASH TV

Hailing from Essex herself, Jesy totes adores TOWIE! Her ideal chill-out day is watching the hilare show in her PJs with a pizza. Now who wouldn't enjoy that?

3 THEY'RE SCARED OF STUFF

Yes, even celebs have phobias! Jade is petrified of flying, Jesy hates spiders, Perrie has a fear of rollercoasters and Leigh-Anne can't stand flying insects.

4 THEY LOVE THEIR FAM

The girls couldn't live without their families and know they wouldn't be where they are today without their love and support. No matter how huge they become, fam is always number one. Sound familiar?

5 THEY MOAN ABOUT STUFF

The girls try to have a positive attitude but, like the rest of us, they sometimes need a good old moan! In fact, one of Jesy's nicknames is Whining Willow because she enjoys moaning so much!

6 THEY GET STARSTRUCK

Who knew that celebs get starstruck too? Perrie didn't know what to say when Katy Perry told her she liked her hair and Leigh-Anne once got so starstruck when Justin Beiber stopped to say hi that she couldn't speak at all!

7 THEY HAVE 'NORMAL' HOBBIES

It's not all expensive activities and A-list clubs for these girls. On a rare day off you're more likely to find Jade puzzling over Sudoku and Perrie with a pair of knitting needles in her hands.

8 THEY KNOW HOW TO HAVE A LAUGH

OMG, these girls know how to LOL! When you see them messing around and making each other giggle doesn't it just remind you of you and your mates having a laugh?

9 THEY SHOP HIGH STREET

They may be designer label kweeens on the red carpet but the girls still wear high street too. Zara is one of Jade's fave shops and Perrie gets her fash on at Top Shop.

10 THEY HAVE 'NORMAL' FRIENDS

The girls are all each other's BBFs obvs, but they're still close to their friends from life before Little Mix too. When they head home they can't wait to catch up with them for a good old natter.

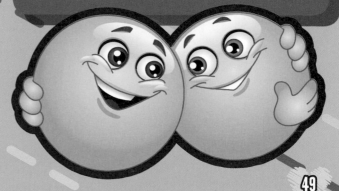

Say WHAT?

Design your own hilare Little Mix emojis. It's all about the feels.

You've totally nailed the aesthetic!

CREATE A FACE EMOJI FOR EACH MIXER.

JESY LEIGH-ANNE JADE PERRIE

DESIGN AN ICON TO REPRESENT EACH GROUP MEMBER.

JESY LEIGH-ANNE JADE PERRIE

TOP Tip

Think about the girls' fave things.

Own it!

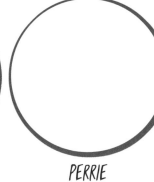

DRAW WHAT YOUR FACE WOULD LOOK LIKE IF YOU MET LITTLE MIX.

Screeeeeeam!!!

CREATE A FIERCE ICON FOR YOUR FAVOURITE LITTLE MIX SONG.

Smashed it!

DOODLE SOME EMOJIS OR ICONS FOR THESE MOMENTOUS LITTLE MIX MOMENTS.

NEED SOME INSPO?

Use this emoji creation kit to give you some ideas.

THE GIRLS' LATEST SINGLE TOPS THE CHARTS #WOOHOO

LITTLE MIX WIN AN AWARD #HURRAY

PERRIE GETS A NEW PUPPY #SOCUTE

JADE GETS A NEW BOO #AWWW

Are you MANAGEMENT Material?

Think you could boss being Little Mix's manager? Take this fun quiz to find out if you've got what it takes!

1 What's on the girls' agenda today?

A Recording a new single.

B A live performance.

C A chill-out day.

2 What will they wear?

A Cool but casual - you make sure they're always prepared for the paps.

B Super-glam - red carpet ready is the look you're going for.

C Comfy cosy - you want them to feel happy and relaxed.

3 What are their evening plans?

A A quick PA then an early night so they're refreshed for tomorrow.

B They've got an invitation to the hottest celeb party in town - with a plus one.

C A fun sleepover - and you're invited too.

4 What's on the lunch menu?

A A healthy salad in the studio.

B A meal at a fancy restaurant.

C A takeaway at yours.

5

What's the last text you'll send the girls today?

A A thank you and well done for all their hard work today. ☐

B A request to introduce you to one of their celeb pals. ☐

C The deets for a fun activity for you all on their next day off. ☐

6

What are you gonna post on their socials?

A A sneak peak of their new video. ☐

B A behind-the-scenes selfie of you and the girls. ☐

C A pic of your fave album cover. ☐

7

How would the girls describe you?

A Organised. ☐

B Outgoing. ☐

C Friendly. ☐

Mostly As - Bossing It!

You're friendly but professional, fun but firm. Although you're a big Little Mix fan, you'd always put their career above anything else. You would make the perf celeb manager - when can you start?

Mostly Bs - Wannabe Star!

You like to get your fash on and be seen in all the right places. A management role is just too behind-the-scenes for a rising star like you. Maybe you should start looking for a manager of your own instead?

Mostly Cs - Stan Fan!

You've totally smashed it as a superfan but you like Little Mix way too much to be their manager. You'd just want to spend all day hanging out together! If there's ever an opening for their BFF though, be sure to apply!

ON THE MAP

Let's take a trip around the UK to visit some of the places that put Little Mix on the map. Buckle up and off we go!

GLASGOW

Perrie auditioned for *The X Factor* in this Scottish city after the audition she'd been planning to go to in Newcastle was cancelled at the last minute. Her Mam woke her up at 4am to drive her there and the rest, as they say, is history!

HIGH WYCOMBE

Leigh-Anne grew up in this Buckinghamshire town. She still heads home for visits and once the High Wycombe branch of River Island - Leigh's fave shop - opened up exclusively for her! That's taking customer service to a whole new level!

CORNWALL

A young Jesy lived on the Cornish coast for a while until the fam moved back to Essex. Jesy remembers the house having a big winding staircase that their mum would let them slide down on a mattress! Best. Mum. Ever.

NEWCASTLE

Perrie was studying performing arts at college here when she auditioned for *The X Factor*. If pop superstardom hadn't worked out for her, plan b was to be a drama teacher.

NOTTING HILL, LONDON

When Little Mix first won *The X Factor*, northern girls Perrie and Jade made the move south to London. They'd heard of Notting Hill (because of the film of the same name!) so they decided to move there. Almost a decade later, all four girls still live in or near the big smoke.

SOUTH SHIELDS

Both Perrie and Jade hail from this North East town. Perrie remembers moving around a lot as a child but, apart from 18 months in New Zealand, South Shields has always been home.

CAMDEN, LONDON

When Jade, Leigh-Anne, Jesy and Jade were first put together as a group, their mums gave them money to go to Camden and buy their outfits for *The X Factor*. The girls splashed their cash on matching stripy vest tops and socks - adorbs!

ROMFORD

Jesy calls this Essex town home. And before you ask, no it isn't where TOWIE is filmed!

WEYMOUTH

Perrie has family here and spending time in this pretty seaside town is her fave way to unwind. When she's in Weymouth she loves doing simple things like walking her dogs. Sounds like the perf celeb getaway.

PUTNEY, LONDON

Jesy and Leigh-Anne shared a penthouse apartment here in the early days of Little Mix. With a huge open-plan living area, massive balcony and speakers in the ceiling it was the perfect party pad. We feel sorry for their neighbours!

Positive VIBES

The girls know that if things get you down, positivity can boost you back up again. Here's how to stay positive the Little Mix way.

5 rules for POSITIVE THINKING

TALK IT OUT
KEEPING NEGATIVE FEELINGS BOTTLED UP IS NEVER A GOOD IDEA.

DON'T DWELL ON THINGS
DEAL WITH ANYTHING THAT'S BOTHERING YOU THEN LET IT GO.

PUT THINGS INTO PERSPECTIVE
IT'S USUALLY NOT AS BAD AS YOU THINK.

LIVE IN THE MOMENT
TRY NOT TO WORRY ABOUT WHAT MIGHT HAPPEN IN THE FUTURE.

SMILE
THE SIMPLE ACT OF SMILING (EVEN IF YOU DON'T FEEL LIKE IT) CAN MAKE YOU FEEL HAPPIER, AND THAT'S A SCIENTIFIC FACT!

you got this!

LOVE YOUR LIFE

There are some things in life that you have to do whether you want to or not (go to school, come home on time, keep your room tidy blah, blah, blah) but when you get the choice of how to spend your time, do something you love. The Little Mix girls found their passion in singing – where will you find yours?

iT'S GONNA Be OKAY

KEEP ON TRYING

If you really want something, don't give up, even if things get a little hard along the way. Stay positive and keep trying. Imagine if Jade had never auditioned for *The X-Factor* again after getting sent home from boot camp not once, but twice. There. Would. Be. No. Little. Mix. Imagine that!

think POSITIVE

FIND YOUR POSITIVE INSPO

Look to other people for positive inspiration in your life. It could be a friend, a teacher or even a celebrity, as long as they have qualities you admire. The Little Mix girls have a whole host of inspos (see pages 32-33) so if you're having trouble choosing, just borrow one of theirs!

Stay POSITIVE

Try these five mood-boosting activities when you need some feel-good fun.

Spread KiNDNESS

(see pages 32-33)

LOL Lessons!

1 SING
ALONG TO YOUR FAVOURITE TRACK AT THE TOP OF YOUR VOICE – DON'T WORRY IF YOU'RE OUT OF TUNE!

2 BAKE
YOURSELF A YUMMY TREAT THEN ENJOY EVERY MOUTHFUL.

3 WATCH
YOUR FAVOURITE HAPPY MOVIE WITH YOUR BFF.

4 TREAT YO'SELF!
PAINT YOUR NAILS, DO YOUR HAIR, PUT ON A FACEMASK – WHATEVER MAKES YOU FEEL GOOD.

5 CHILL-OUT
WITH A GOOD BOOK/IN A WARM BUBBLE BATH/ WATCHING YOUR FAVE BOXSET

ViRTUAL HUG

HAVE A GOOD GIGGLE

Laughing can really boost your mood so surround yourself with people who make you happy. Luckily for the Little Mixers they find each other hilare so when they're together the positive vibes just keep on flowing!

Eat Like Little Mix!

Follow these simple steps to create Leigh-Anne's fave comfort food – nachos with all the trimmings. Delish!

YOU WILL NEED

- ♡ LARGE BAG OF NACHOS
- ♡ 100G CHEESE
- ♡ TOPPINGS OF YOUR CHOICE
- ♡ SOURED CREAM

How to make

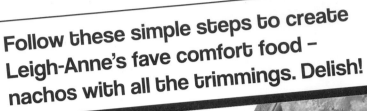

ADULT GUIDANCE IS NEEDED FOR THIS ACTIVITY.

1 Pre-heat the oven to 180°C (160°C for fan ovens)/350°F/Gas mark 4.

2 Empty the nachos onto an ovenproof plate or tray.

3 Grate the cheese and scatter over the nachos.

4 Add your toppings of choice.

TOPPING IDEAS

♡ SALSA

♡ GUACAMOLE

♡ SLICED CHILLI

♡ SLICED OLIVES

5 Heat in the oven for about 10 minutes, or until the cheese has melted, then carefully take the nachos out using oven gloves as the plate/tray will be hot.

6 Transfer your nachos onto a plate if necessary, top with soured cream and enjoy!

Nachos are perf for sharing!

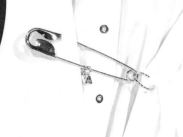

MMMMMM!

Leigh-Anne's fave nacho toppings are pico de gallo (a chunky Mexican salsa) and guacamole.

Hidden TRACKS

Put on some choons, turn up the volume and find the LM5 songs below hidden in this supersize wordsearch.

A	C	W	F	L	O	V	E	A	G	I	R	L	R	I	G	H	T	O	F
G	W	O	M	A	N	L	I	K	E	M	E	J	H	E	O	S	H	N	B
J	F	A	L	R	S	E	W	H	M	D	A	W	O	N	S	A	O	J	S
O	P	T	R	S	S	U	T	U	O	B	A	K	N	I	H	T	S	A	H
A	D	I	O	Q	E	I	F	H	M	S	Q	K	G	F	I	G	J	E	L
N	D	S	P	L	A	R	W	P	D	S	T	H	E	C	U	R	E	W	H
O	P	F	W	A	D	S	N	D	A	T	D	W	E	K	S	I	S	K	L
F	G	A	S	D	A	Y	M	L	G	R	F	F	G	Y	P	M	S	R	T
A	O	E	P	R	W	F	O	Y	R	I	H	Y	P	S	R	O	T	W	P
R	D	M	F	I	G	H	S	U	Q	P	M	K	G	J	P	R	Y	T	Y
C	G	N	J	O	D	K	R	T	S	H	D	K	A	W	S	E	C	D	O
P	S	I	L	O	V	E	G	E	V	O	N	O	S	A	S	T	H	D	B
H	J	R	U	I	R	F	T	G	M	X	A	J	P	D	G	H	O	U	N
L	P	E	F	J	T	A	K	W	A	S	A	B	I	P	Y	A	A	P	A
L	D	T	K	S	V	L	D	L	G	O	A	S	J	H	G	N	C	F	C
P	O	S	S	I	F	A	O	D	W	E	H	P	F	R	O	W	H	D	I
K	D	N	T	S	F	E	R	S	F	J	T	E	F	Y	L	O	O	D	R
F	S	O	T	F	O	R	G	E	T	Y	O	U	N	O	T	R	H	D	E
S	M	M	F	C	A	S	H	T	F	S	R	N	P	S	V	D	P	F	M
D	A	S	O	N	L	Y	Y	O	U	D	P	E	S	A	W	S	T	S	A

- ☐ WOMAN LIKE ME
- ☐ MOTIVATE
- ☐ AMERICAN BOY
- ☐ THINK ABOUT US
- ☐ TOLD YOU SO
- ☐ ONLY YOU
- ☐ JOAN OF ARC
- ☐ THE CURE
- ☐ NOTICE
- ☐ FORGET YOU NOT
- ☐ MORE THAN WORDS
- ☐ WASABI
- ☐ MONSTER IN ME
- ☐ LOVE A GIRL RIGHT
- ☐ STRIP

Answers on pages 76-77.

Dream

Steal her Style...
LEIGH-ANNE

Leigh-Anne totally bosses fierce fashion.

Get the look
LOOK FOR **BOLD** COLOURS, **UNUSUAL** DESIGNS, **FITTED** DRESSES, **TAILORED** TROUSERS AND **COORDINATING** ACCESSORIES.

Puffy sleeves are so hot right now!

Check out the matching bag!

Leigh-Anne looks like she means business in this pinstripe shirt dress.

Pale, thigh high boots soften the look.

FAVE

HIGH STREET *shop*

RIVER ISLAND

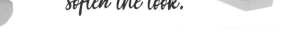

Stripes are totally trending at the mo so full fash points to Leigh-Anne!

The electric blue layer adds a pop of colour to this LBD.

Dusky pink looks perf on Leigh-Anne as this gorge outfit proves.

This daring green suit with lace AND bows is all kinds of awesome!

Leigh-Anne has smashed it with this brightly coloured playsuit.

♡ Must-Have Item
BLACK LEATHER CLUTCH BAG.

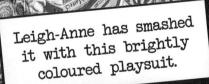

Steal her Style... JESY

Jesy rocks the alternative look.

Get the look
BAGGY BOTTOMS, ANIMAL PRINT, COLOUR POPS, FITTED TOPS AND SIMPLE ACCESSORIES.

The asymmetric style adds a touch of daytime glam.

Will ripped jeans ever go out of fash? We hope not!

Simple white boots complete this cool-casual look.

High waisted jeans are totally on point.

FAVE

HIGH STREET shop

TOP SHOP

Jesy looks très chic in this black ensemble with matching beret!

Jesy nails it in snake print and neon - a winning combo!

Oversized tops teamed with casual camo is Jesy's trademark look.

Don't worry, Jesy hasn't lost her shoes a la Cinderella! Look closely and you'll see she's sporting a cool transparent pair.

Jesy is red carpet ready in this eye-catching orange gown.

Must-Have Item
AN OVERSIZED HOODY.

Steal her Style...

 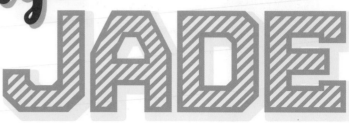

JADE

Cool and cute is Jade's signature style.

Get the look
THINK **BOYFRIEND** JEANS,
OVERSIZED HOODIES,
KILLER HEELS, **SIMPLE**
STYLES AND **CUTE**
ACCESSORIES.

*Retro tie die
is soooooo hot
right now.*

*Who doesn't
love a good
slogan?*

*Turn-ups
give Jade's
jeans a whole
new look.*

*Loosely tied
Docs complete
the laid-back
vibe.*

★ *FAVE* ★

HIGH STREET *shop*

ZARA

Jade scrubs up well in this stylish black trouser suit.

Jade's floor length train adds a touch of elegance to this award show outfit.

What's better than a slogan? A sequin slogan of course!

Gold is Jade's colour as proven by this beaut of a dress!

Must-Have Item
A SLOGAN TEE

Casual but stylish is what Jade does best.

WORK HARD DREAM BIG

Steal her Style...

 **PERRIE**

 GRL PWR

 love you

Get the look
EXPERIMENT WITH **VINTAGE** ITEMS, HAIR **ACCESSORIES**, **LAYERS**, **FLOATY** SKIRTS AND **SOFT** FABRICS.

The trusty denim jacket never goes out of fash.

This stripy shirt dress is so Perrie.

The belt nips Perrie's loose dress in at the waist.

Coordinating long boots tie the whole outfit together.

 **FAVE**

HIGH STREET shop

URBAN OUTFITTERS

Perrie is dressed to impress in this little black number.

Perrie loves a good piece of headwear.

Bright white looks clean and fresh but what's with the super long sleeves?!

This simple trouser suits screams sophistication.

♡Must-Have Item♡
A HAIRBAND

Perrie does double denim to perfection with this cute daytime look.

Jesy

Copper toned eyeshadow works well with Jesy's bright orange dress.

Nude lips balance out the dramatic eyes.

Huge lashes are Jesy's make-up must-have.

Make-up GOALS

Jade

Jade's brows are groomed to perfection.

Highlighter gives Jade's skin a natural dewy look.

Pale pink eyeshadow with black liquid liner is a winning combo.

Perfectly applied blusher defines Perrie's cheekbones.

Neutral lippy works well with Perrie's skin tone.

The smoky eye is a really flattering lewk.

PERRIE

Glowing skin, perfectly tamed eyebrows and dramatic lashes are all part of the Little Mix Lewk.

Bronzer adds a healthy glow to Leigh-Anne's cheeks.

LEIGH-ANNE

Understated lipstick makes the eyes really stand out.

Liquid eyeliner creates the perfect flick.

Get the LM LOOK

Wanna have locks like Little Mix? Then read on to find out how to get the girls' signature styles.

JADE'S LOOSE WAVES

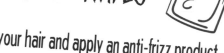

1. Wash your hair and apply an anti-frizz product.
2. While your hair is still damp, braid it into two plaits.
3. Leave overnight or until your hair is completely dry.
4. Take the plaits out and carefully separate your hair with your fingers tips.
5. Spritz with seasalt spray and you're good to go.

LEIGH-ANNE'S DRAMATIC CURLS

1. Use an anti-frizz shampoo to wash your hair.
2. Smooth a curl cream or serum through your hair from roots to ends.
3. Dry your hair in sections using a diffuser attachment on the end of your hairdryer. If you don't have a diffuser, scrunch your hair as you blow dry it.
4. Once your hair is completely dry, rub a squirt of serum between your palms run your hands through the curls.
5. If you want extra definition, take small sections of hair and twist them around your finger to make corkscrew curls.

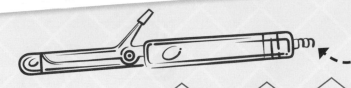

If your hair is naturally straight, you'll need to use tongs to create your curls.

LITTLE MIX

JESY'S SLEEK AND STRAIGHT STYLE

1. After washing your hair, smooth an anti-frizz product through to the ends.

2. Divide the hair into sections and dry on a high heat using a big round brush. Curl each section of hair around the brush and run the hairdryer nozzle down the length of the hair to dry it straight.

3. Once your hair is completely dry, spritz it with a heat protector spray.

4. Set your hair straighteners to a high heat and divide your hair into sections. Carefully run the straighteners down the length of each section from root to ends.

5. Once you've straightened every section of hair, smooth a tiny amount of serum through to tame any flyaway strands.

Make sure you trim your ends regularly for healthy looking hair!

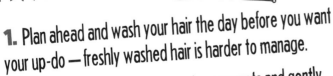

PERRIE'S UP-DO

1. Plan ahead and wash your hair the day before you want your up-do — freshly washed hair is harder to manage.

2. Spray a little dry shampoo onto your roots and gently back comb to create volume.

3. Brush your hair into a high pony tail, leaving some strands hanging loose at the front, and tie with a hairband.

4. Loosely twist your pony tail and wrap it around the hairband. Fix in place using hair grips.

5. Use hair straighteners to straighten the loose strands around your face then fix everything in place with a blast of hairspray.

HAIRSPRAY

Are you a MEGA MIXER?

Just how much do you like Little Mix? Take our fun fan quiz to find out once and for all!

1 How many Little Mix albums do you own?

A All of them in at least one format.

B I've got my faves.

C None.

2 How many LM posters are on your bedroom walls?

A So many I've lost count.

B At least five.

C None.

3 Do you know all the lyrics to your fave LM song?

A Of course! I reckon I could even sing it backwards!

B I know the chorus – does that count?

C No, I just hum along.

4 Do you like to dress like your favourite Little Mixer?

A Almost every outfit I own is based on their wardrobe.

B I have some clothes that look a bit like what they'd wear.

C I'd rather look like myself, thank you very much.

5 If you saw the girls walking down the street IRL what would you do?

A Scream, take a selfie then pass out with excitement!

B Take a sneaky pic while pretending to reply to a text.

C Play it cool and just walk on by.

Mostly As – Superfan!

You live and breathe Little Mix and probably know more about the girls than they do themselves! You love their music, follow their fash and own all the merch. You're 100% obsessed and you don't care who knows it!

Mostly Bs – Chilled Fan!

You like Little Mix's music and would defo hit the dancefloor if your fave track came on but you're not obsessed with the girls. You're a chilled fan rather than a stan and that suits you just fine!

Mostly Cs – Not Fussed!

You might hum along to a Little Mix hit but you're not fussed enough about their music to call yourself a fan. And you definitely wouldn't try to steal their style! This book probably doesn't even belong to you!

#WATCH THIS SPACE

What will the Little Mixers be up to in the future? Let's take a peek at some of their plans.

TALENT SPOTTING

The girls were due to start filming a brand new BBC talent show when the coronavirus lockdown put their plans on hold. *Little Mix The Search* will see Leigh-Anne, Perrie, Jesy and Jade turn mentors as they look for singers to form a new band. The show sounds all kinds of awesome and, when it finally airs, we're sure it will be worth the wait.

TV DOC

Rumours are flying around that another Little Mixer will soon be presenting a BBC documentary. Following in the footsteps of Jesy with her award-winning doc *Odd One Out*, the BBC have apparently teamed up with Leigh-Anne to make a programme highlighting the issues of racism in the UK. We can't think of anyone better placed to shine the spotlight on this important subject. Let's hope that for once the rumours are true!

GOING LIVE

Riding high on the success of their LM5 Tour, Little Mix announced they would tour again in the summer of 2020 with the appropriately named Summer 2020 Tour! The girls were gutted when they had to cancel the 21-date tour because of social distancing rules in place due to coronavirus. Fingers crossed another tour will be scheduled soon.

AND THE REST!

It's a fair guess to say there will also be single releases, TV appearances, new merch and much, much more. As they say, watch this space. Whatever the girls have up their sleeves is sure to be awesome!

ANSWERS

Pages 16-17
CHANGES CHALLENGE

Pages 30-31
WHOSE WARDROBE?

A - Jade.

B - Leigh-Anne.

C - Jesy.

D - Perrie.

Spread **KiNDNESS**

Page 34
SONG SNIPPETS

1. Woman Like Me.

2. DNA.

3. One I've Been Missing.

4. Black Magic.

5. Cannonball.

6. Bounce Back.

7. Shout Out To My Ex.

8. Break Up Song.

Page 35
X WORD FUN!

Page 38
SONG SCRAMBLE

1. Wasabi.

2. Woman Like Me.

3. Power.

4. Black Magic.

5. Think About Us.

6. Bounce Back.

7. Only You.

8. No More Sad Songs.

Stay POSITIVE

A	C	W	F	L	O	V	E	A	G	I	R	L	R	I	G	H	T	O	F
G	W	O	M	A	N	L	I	K	E	M	E	J	H	E	O	S	H	N	B
J	F	A	L	R	S	E	W	H	M	D	A	W	O	N	S	A	O	J	S
O	P	T	R	S	S	U	T	U	O	B	A	K	N	I	H	T	S	A	H
A	D	I	O	Q	E	I	F	H	M	S	Q	K	G	F	I	G	J	E	L
N	D	S	P	L	A	R	W	P	D	S	T	H	E	C	U	R	E	W	H
O	P	F	W	A	D	S	N	D	A	T	D	W	E	K	S	I	S	K	L
F	G	A	S	D	A	Y	M	L	G	R	F	F	G	Y	P	M	S	R	T
A	O	E	P	R	W	F	O	Y	R	I	H	Y	P	S	R	O	T	W	P
R	D	M	F	I	G	H	S	U	Q	P	M	K	G	J	P	R	Y	T	Y
C	G	N	J	O	D	K	R	T	S	H	D	K	A	W	S	E	C	D	O
P	S	I	L	O	V	E	G	E	V	O	N	O	S	A	S	T	H	D	B
H	J	R	U	I	R	F	T	G	M	X	A	J	P	D	G	H	O	U	N
L	P	E	F	J	T	A	K	W	A	S	A	B	I	P	Y	A	A	P	A
L	D	T	K	S	V	L	D	L	G	O	A	S	J	H	G	N	C	F	C
P	O	S	S	I	F	A	O	D	W	E	H	P	F	R	O	W	H	D	I
K	D	N	T	S	F	E	R	S	F	J	T	E	F	Y	L	O	O	D	R
F	S	O	T	F	O	R	G	E	T	Y	O	U	N	O	T	R	H	D	E
S	M	M	F	C	A	S	H	T	F	S	R	N	P	S	V	D	P	F	M
D	A	S	O	N	L	Y	Y	O	U	D	P	E	S	A	W	S	T	S	A

77

PICTURE CREDITS